BEAST

Susan Meddaugh

Houghton Mifflin Company Boston 1981

For Vicki Moran

Library of Congress Cataloging in Publication Data
Meddaugh, Susan.
    Beast.

    SUMMARY: Anna's family plans to destroy a big,
furry beast that comes out of the forest, but Anna is
not convinced it's dangerous.
    [1. Monsters—Fiction]   I. Title.
PZ7.M51273Be   [E]   80-24851
ISBN 0-395-30349-4

Printed in the United States of America.
 P 10 9 8 7 6 5 4 3 2 1

Anna saw it first.
It was big and furry, and it
came out of the forest.

"What is it?" said Anna to her family.
Father and Mother, Raymond, Reba, and Robert
all looked up.
"It's bigger than a bear," they cried, "and
worse than a wolf."
They had never seen anything like it before.

Mother said, "A beast that ugly must be
very bad."

Father went hunting for the beast.
It got away.
"A beast that tricky must be very
dangerous," said Father.

That night the shadow of the beast stretched out
across the ground.

"A beast that big must be very strong," said Robert.

"A beast that big must be ferocious," said Reba.

"A beast that big must be completely fearless," said
Raymond.

He blew out the candle.

9

"Everybody knows about the beast
except me," said Anna.

"I will find out some things for
myself," she said.

"First, I will find out if a beast that big is hungry."

CLOMP! CLOMP! CLOMP!

CHOMP! CHOMP! CHOMP!

"What's that noise?" asked Mother and Father.

"What's that noise?" asked Raymond, Reba, and Robert.

"It's the beast," said Anna.

"The beast is at the door!" they gasped.

"It's mean and dangerous!" cried Mother and Father.

"It's strong! Ferocious! Fearless!" cried Robert, Reba, and Raymond.

"And it's very hungry," said Anna proudly.

17

They made so much noise that the beast ran away.

It ran into the barn.

"Quick," said Mother. "Close the barn door."

"TRAP THE BEAST!" they shouted.
"LOCK IT IN THE BARN!"

Then they climbed a ladder to the loft.

They crept up to the edge of the loft.
They peeked over.
"A beast that terrible must be destroyed,"
they said.

But the night was dark, and the beast
was scary.
"I'll do it tomorrow," said Father.

"Poor beast," thought Anna.
When the others left, she stayed behind.

"Beast," said Anna, "I'd like
to help, but you are so mean
and dangerous that you must be
destroyed."

"Still," she said, "I wish I
knew more about you."
She leaned out over the
edge.

"Oh!" said Anna, as she fell
from the loft.

"Ummph," she said as she
landed on something big and
soft . . . and warm.

"MMoomph," said the beast.

"OOOWWWOOWW," cried the beast.
"Oh dear," said Anna. "Did I hurt you?"

"A beast as big and strong as you are
should not cry."

"OOOWWWOOWW," howled the beast.

"Now, now," said Anna. "A beast as ferocious
and fearless as you are should not be afraid."

"There, there," Anna soothed.

Then she said, "A beast this nice must be protected."

She opened the barn door.

"Good-bye, beast," said Anna. "And don't come back."

The next morning, Anna's family got a surprise.
The barn was empty.
The beast was gone.
"I *knew* that evil beast was tricky," said Father.
But Anna just smiled.
For she was the only one who knew the beast
at all.